PHYSICS

A Hair is Wider Than a MILLION ATOMS

Dr. Bryson Gore

Stargazer Books

CONTENTS

© Aladdin Books Ltd 2006

Designed and produced by
Aladdin Books Ltd

First published in the
United States in 2006 by
Stargazer Books
c/o The Creative Company
123 South Broad Street
P.O. Box 227
Mankato, Minnesota 56002

Printed in Malaysia

Editor: Katie Harker
Design: Flick, Book Design
and Graphics
Picture Research:
Brian Hunter Smart
Illustrators: Q2A Creative

The author, Dr. Bryson Gore, is
a freelance lecturer and science
demonstrator, working with the
Royal Institution and other
science centers in the UK.

Library of Congress Cataloging-in-
Publication Data

Gore, Bryson.
    Physics / by Bryson Gore.
        p. cm. -- (Wow science)
    Includes index.
    ISBN 1-59604-067-X
    1. Physics--Juvenile
    literature. I. Title.

QC25.G67 2005
530--dc22
                            2004058619

Introduction

Humans have puzzled over PHYSICS—the behavior of matter—for hundreds of thousands of years. How do light and sound travel? Why do some materials break? What is magnetism? Over time, we have found out many things about the nature of our world—but many secrets of physics still lie waiting to be discovered.

In ancient times, people believed that the behavior of the world around us could be attributed to the actions of the gods—and few tests were ever conducted to oppose these ideas. It wasn't until the 17th century AD that physical principles began to be openly discussed and rigorously tested. Soon scientists, like Galileo, undertook experiments to justify physical theories and to create new laws about the natural world.

The 17th century saw the proposal by Isaac Newton that matter was made up of particles. This theory led to scientific attempts across the globe to find simple patterns that would help to explain the complex nature of matter. In the 19th century, John Dalton named these particles "atoms," and the scientist Johannes van der Waals discovered how small these atoms were. In 1910, van der Waals was awarded the Nobel Prize in Physics for his work.

Newton also developed a series of mathematical laws that changed the way that people understood forces and motion—enabling scientists to make new measurements and physical predictions of their own. As each century has progressed, the breakthroughs of eminent scientists have encouraged other physicists to try their hand at explaining the complex nature of things. And so the story continues today.

This book takes a look at twelve of the most amazing developments in physical science that have taken place through history. Find out more about famous physicists like Galileo and Newton and learn how they used their skills to make sense of the world around them. By consulting fact boxes such as "The science of..." and "How do we know?," you will begin to understand more about the ways in which we have pieced together the story of forces, energy, and matter. Learn about the effects of gravity, the causes of friction, and the properties of everyday materials— that together explain the nature of our physical world.

WHEN YOU WALK TO THE WEST THE EARTH SPINS FASTER

Whenever you move around—by walking, running, or turning—you use forces to change the way you are moving. In fact, these forces also change the way that the earth is moving. Rather like walking on a slow-moving treadmill, the force of our movement may sometimes coincide (or counteract) with the direction of the earth's spin.

In ancient times, people thought that the earth was sitting still at the center of the universe. This was because they couldn't feel any effects that indicated that the earth was moving. In fact, the earth feels stationary in just the same way that an airplane (moving at a constant speed) feels stationary—we can move about inside a plane without even noticing that it is moving. Similarly, because the whole solar system is moving at an almost constant speed through space, we feel no effect.

West

THE SCIENCE OF...

Whenever you move around you are accelerating yourself—speeding up, slowing down, and changing direction. In each case a force is needed to create these changes in motion. But forces that change the way you are moving also have an impact on the object that you are pushing against. For example, when you paddle in a row boat, the force of your paddle pushes the boat forward and ALSO pushes the water backward.

We know from our studies of the solar system that the earth rotates (spins around) once a day. If you were in a spaceship looking down at the North Pole, you would see that the earth is spinning in a counterclockwise direction (see main image). If you stand at the equator (the extreme point of the earth's rotation) like the girl, you would actually be traveling at 25,000 miles (40,000 km) every 24 hours (about 1,056 mph / 1,700 km/h). That's about twice the speed of a jumbo jet!

If you begin to walk to the west you are pushing in the same direction as the earth's rotation, forcing the earth to speed up. If you walk to the east, you are opposing the earth's rotation and forcing the earth to slow down—of course, only by a small amount.

Earth's rotation

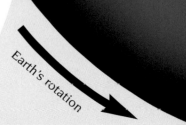

HOW DO WE KNOW?

For thousands of years scientists were very confused about the way in which objects moved—and generally got it wrong! Then, in the 17th century, the scientist Sir Isaac Newton declared that there were three rules, or laws, that explained motion:

1 An object will continue to sit still or travel in a straight line, at a constant speed, unless a force makes it change.
2 For a given force, the change in motion will be bigger for small (light) objects and smaller for heavy ones.
3 The force will affect both the object that is pushed AND the object that is doing the pushing.

So, a boat on a lake will sit still until somebody, or something, pushes it. It's much easier to make an empty boat move than one that has people sitting in it. If you are standing on the bank when you push the boat it just moves away, but if you are sitting in another boat then you will find that your boat moves backward as the other boat moves away.

The third law is the most difficult one to understand because we normally stand on a non-slippery surface when we push on a very heavy object. What we don't realize is that we are actually pushing in two directions at once! We push the object in one direction and the earth in the other—the earth is so much heavier that we cannot detect the fact that it changes speed.

West East

YOU WEIGH LESS WHEN THE MOON IS OVERHEAD

There are lots of myths about the human body. "You weigh less in the morning," "You are shorter in the evening." But how true are some of these claims? When it comes to weight, scientists can certainly prove that changing positions of the moon can influence the amount that we weigh on the scales.

THE SCIENCE OF...

How much do you weigh? In a spacecraft you can be weightless, on the surface of the moon you'd weigh about a sixth of what you weigh on Earth, and if you stood on the surface of the sun you'd weigh nearly thirty times as much!

How can your weight change depending upon where you are? The answer is that your mass—how much stuff you're made from—stays the same but your weight depends on the force of gravity. On the surface of the earth, gravity pulls each kilogram (kg) of mass down with a force of 9.8 newtons (N). This means that a person with a mass of 110 pounds (50 kg) is pulled down toward the earth with a force of about 500 newtons. That's why when you jump, you come back down to Earth again! An apple has a weight on Earth of about 1 newton.

When the moon is directly overhead we are pulled by the gravity of both the earth and the moon. The moon is both smaller than the earth and much farther away. Therefore it has a weaker force of gravity—about 30 millionths of a newton per kilogram. However, the moon still changes your weight by about one thousandth of a newton each day. Although the moon's effect on a person is barely measurable, we can see the moon's effect on the oceans. When the moon is overhead, the surface of the sea rises and this is what causes the tides.

HOW DO WE KNOW?

Sir Isaac Newton realized that all objects are attracted to each other by gravity. He proposed a law of gravity stating that the gravitational force between two objects was G x (Mass1/distance) x (Mass2/distance). Although the mass of each object and the distance between them was known, no one knew the value of the gravitational constant ("G"). Newton managed to show that all objects —from apples falling to Earth, to the earth orbiting the sun—used the same value of "G," but he didn't know what "G" was!

In 1798, Henry Cavendish successfully worked out the value of "G" by measuring the force of gravity between two suspended balls of lead. Our knowledge of the gravitational constant means that we can now calculate the force between two people. If you weigh about 130 lbs (60 kg) and stand next to someone of a similar build, you will be attracted by a force of about one millionth of a newton.

Two tides move across the oceans each day. This is because, as the earth rotates, different points of the earth (and the water on it) are being pulled by the moon's gravity. On the nearside of the earth, water closest to the moon is pulled by the moon's gravity to form a "high tide." The water on the farside of the earth is also at high tide because the moon's gravity pulls the earth away from the water.

Light and sound are both types of waves. Sound travels at about 984 feet per second (300 m/s) through air, but light travels at about 186,000 miles per second (300,000 km/s)—that's a foot (30 cm) in a billionth of a second!

Light is produced by the interaction of electricity and magnetism and does not need anything to travel through. It is for this reason that light travels through a vacuum (empty space) although sound does not. Light travels slightly slower in air than it does in outer space, but in things like glass and water the speed drops to about 124,000 miles per second (200,000 km/s). In diamonds, the speed can fall to around 78,000 miles per second (125,000 km/s). Today, the speed of light in a vacuum is defined to be exactly 186,282 miles per second (299,792.458 km/s).

Sound travels because of the compression (squeezing together) and rarefraction (stretching apart) of the atoms and molecules in a material through which the sound is traveling. Sound generally travels faster in solids and liquids than in air. The atoms in solids and liquids are closer together than in gases, so the compression is transferred from one place to another more quickly. The speed of sound in water is about 4,900 feet/sec (1,500 m/s) and in solids like glass and steel the speed rises to around 3 miles per second (5 km/s).

LIGHT TRAVELS A MILLION TIMES FASTER THAN SOUND

Have you ever wondered why the flash of lightning always happens before the roll of thunder? In fact, the flash and the roll occur at the same time, but the light travels to our eyes almost instantly. If the lightning occurs 1.86 miles (3 km) away, then the light reaches us in one hundred thousandth of a second. But the sound of thunder (the air expanding as it is heated by the electricity in the lightning's spark) will take about 10 seconds to cover the same distance.

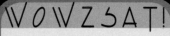

HOW DO WE KNOW?

You can measure the speed of sound using echoes. Stand about 160-330 feet (50-100 meters) away from a flat wall and clap your hands regularly so that each clap is in time with the echo of the previous one. The number of claps that you do in ten seconds, multiplied by twice the distance to the wall and divided by ten, is equivalent to the speed of sound in air.

The speed of light was first measured in almost the same way by Galileo in 1600. Galileo flashed a lantern and an assistant on a faraway hill flashed his own lantern as soon as he saw it. Sadly, all that Galileo could say was that light traveled very fast!

Today, scientists measure the distance from the earth to the moon (or the planets) by timing "echoes" of light. Astronauts who went to the moon left a mirror on the surface—and we can fire a pulse of light at the moon that is reflected back to us on Earth. Calculations have shown that it takes about 2 $\frac{1}{2}$ seconds for light to travel there and back. So the moon is approximately 233,000 miles (375,000 km) away.

Sir Isaac Newton was the first scientist to pass light through a prism and realize that white light, from the sun, was actually a mixture of all the colors of the rainbow—a spectrum of pure colors that could not be broken down any further, but could be recombined into a beam of white light. His experiment also showed that the prism bends blue light the most and red light the least. Why did Newton say that there were seven colors? We now believe that it was simply that seven was his lucky number!

THE SCIENCE OF...

Most of us would be quite sure about the first five colors of the rainbow—but what are indigo and violet? Indigo is the name of the dye that is used to color a pair of jeans and most of us would call that "dark blue." Violet is the color of a flower and most of us would call that a sort of purple. But if you look carefully at a rainbow (or the "spectrum" of colors produced when light shines through a glass prism) you will find that purple doesn't appear anywhere!

A rainbow is produced when light, usually from the sun, is reflected back from raindrops in the air. As the light enters and leaves the drop its direction is changed by an effect called "refraction." Different colors are refracted (have their direction changed) by different amounts. Blue light is refracted the most and red light the least.

A rainbow is an optical illusion and is not really a physical object located in the sky. A rainbow's position is also dependent on where you are looking. We are led to believe that a rainbow has seven colors—including violet but the human eye is not able to detect the color violet (or "purple") in a rainbow or spectrum of light.

How do we know?

Sunlight is made up of hundreds (or thousands) of different pure colors all the way from dark red to dark blue. But humans only have a few names for the colors that are present. If all these colors are present we see white light, if only some are present we see a selection of different colors.

To detect color, humans have three types of cells in their eyes that produce a nerve signal when light falls on them. These three types of cells detect reddish colors of light, greenish light, and bluish light—the three "primary" colors of light. We see red, green, or blue when only one type of cell detects light and gives a signal. If the red and green cells detect light that merges together we see "orangy-yellow;" if the green and blue cells detect light we see "bluey-green;" and if the red and blue cells detect light we see "purple." The human eye is not able to detect the color purple (or "violet") in a rainbow, because red and blue light waves appear at opposite ends of the spectrum (and are not merged).

THERE ARE ONLY SIX COLORS IN THE RAINBOW

Most people have been brought up to recite the colors of the rainbow from memory—red, orange, yellow, green, blue, indigo, and violet. But did you know that violet doesn't actually appear in a rainbow at all? A rainbow is made up of all the colors of the light spectrum—the same colors that we see when white light passes through a glass prism. Violet (or "purple") is a mixture of red and blue light—but this color doesn't exist anywhere in the light spectrum!

MIRRORS DON'T REVERSE LEFT AND RIGHT

Have you thought about the fact that we rarely see ourselves in the way that other people see us? We may catch our reflection in a mirror or a store window—but this is usually a mirror image of ourselves. It's normally only when we look at a photograph of ourselves that we get an accurate portrayal of our own image.

HOW DO WE KNOW?

Look at the picture of the boy looking into a mirror and the mirror image itself. The boy is holding up his right hand but the reflected boy looks like he is holding up his left hand. Has the mirror reversed left and right?

Mirrors don't reverse left and right, but the confusion lies in what we think we are seeing. What you see in the mirror is a "mirror image," but you think that you are seeing an ordinary person who has simply turned around to face you. Left and right are defined in relation to you— imagine a fitness instructor facing you and telling you to raise your left arm while they lift up their right arm. They're pretending to be a mirror image. You are both pointing in the same direction but you are raising different arms. The law of reflection (see page 15) means that if you face a mirror then everything on your left and right will appear on the left and right hand side of the mirror. The same is true for things that are above and below you.

Mirrors actually reverse the direction into and out of the surface of the mirror. If you look into a mirror and point forward, the reflection points backward, toward you. Similarly, when you see a reflection of a landscape in the surface of a calm lake, the angle at which you are looking causes the rays to cross over, turning the image upside down.

We can see our reflection in a mirror because light is reflected back into our eyes. When light hits a rough surface it bounces off at varying angles—and becomes too spread out for us to see, or too distorted to give a clear image. But when light hits a smooth surface, it bounces off at the same angle with which it hit the object. This is known as the "law of reflection" and can be compared to a ball bouncing on the floor—a dropped ball will bounce straight back up, but a ball thrown at an angle will bounce away at the same angle.

Shiny metal surfaces make good mirrors because all the light is reflected. Smooth glass produces a dimmer reflection because most of the light passes through. "Real" objects behind the glass can also overshadow the reflection.

You can make a mirror that reflects in the way that others see you. Tape two mirrors together and stand them at right angles to one another. The paired mirrors produce a double reflection—the second reflection reverses the first reflection and you see a "true" image of yourself.

WOWZAT!

Your image appears upside down in the concave "bowl" of a spoon. This is because the angle of the spoon reflects light rays in a different direction, causing the rays to cross over. This turns your image upside down.

HOW DO WE KNOW?

Atoms are too small to be seen with the naked eye. In fact they're too small to be seen with any microscope that uses light. However, modern microscopes that use electrons to "see" the surface of materials can help us to make images of atoms.

Scientists suspected the existence of atoms long before they were proved to exist. The regular shape of crystals indicated what we now know—that a crystal is a solid in which atoms and molecules are packed in a regularly ordered, repeating pattern. In the 19th century, a Dutch scientist called Johannes van der Waals calculated the size of some atoms by measuring the atomic spacing between pairs of atoms in crystals and by studying the gaseous and liquid states of matter. Van der Waals also discovered that the size of an atom was related to the force of attraction between atoms.

A HAIR IS WIDER THAN A MILLION ATOMS

Everything in the world around us is made from atoms—you, this book, and the ground beneath your feet. Atoms are the smallest bits of any substance and they are tiny! One million atoms sitting side-by-side in a line would be narrower than a human hair. Your hair is made from atoms that have combined to make keratin molecules. It is the twisting long chains of keratin that give your hair its strength.

Today, there are around 115 different elements—92 naturally occuring ones and over 20 that have been artificially created. An atom is the smallest piece of a pure element. Although atoms vary in weight (from hydrogen, the lightest, to darmstadtium which is 281 times heavier), the size of atoms doesn't change that much. Most atoms have a diameter of about a fifth of a millionth of a millimeter.

Atoms are roughly spherical. Although it is hard to be precise about where the "surface" of an atom is, we know that atoms act as if they are very hard because they resist being pushed into each other. So we can think of atoms like tiny marbles or ball bearings. The atoms in metals tend to exist on their own, but many gases and other everyday materials are made from atoms of different elements that combine to form molecules. Water is a molecule made from one oxygen atom and two hydrogen atoms—which is where the chemical name for water, H_2O, comes from.

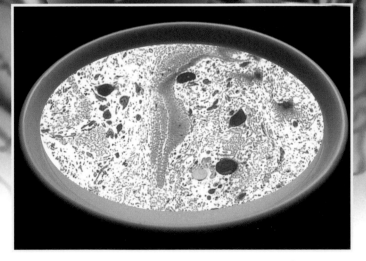

One way to measure the size of large molecules is to float them on the surface of water. If you take a drop of oil about one millimeter across and put it onto the clean surface of a bowl of water it will spread out to form a thin layer (above). We know that the volume of the oil has stayed the same and we can work out that the thickness of the film is about one-tenth of one-thousandth of a millimeter. This is roughly the length of an oil molecule.

IRON WILL BECOME MAGNETIC IF IT IS STRUCK BY LIGHTNING

Magnets are substances that can push or pull on other objects. Some magnets occur naturally while others become magnetic when they come close to other magnets. Lightning is a large electric current formed in clouds that lasts for just a fraction of a second. It produces heat and a strong magnetic field and, for some objects, this is all it takes for magnetism to set to work.

THE SCIENCE OF...

Iron is one of only three pure metals that can make a permanent magnet (the other two are cobalt and nickel). These metals are usually non-magnetic, but if they are "shocked" by being hit or heated up suddenly they can become very strong magnets. If lightning strikes a piece of iron, either a small lump or something as large as a tower, the rapid heating and cooling involved can magnetize it.

We can make mixtures of metals, called "alloys," that include non-magnetic metals that are even stronger magnets than iron. AlNiCo is an alloy of aluminum (which is not normally magnetic) with nickel and cobalt that have been magnetized by heating them up and putting them near to a very strong magnet. Electricity can also be used to make a temporary magnet (or "electromagnet") by wrapping a coil of wire around a piece of iron. The iron becomes temporarily magnetized when an electric current flows through the wire. Electromagnets are useful for lifting large quantities of scrap metal (right) as well as for doorbells and switches.

HOW DO WE KNOW?

The atoms of most metals act like little magnets, but because the atoms point in different directions these magnetic forces cancel themselves out. Certain types of metals and alloys, known as "ferromagnets," can be made to align their atoms and become magnetic. When these atoms are heated, the earth's magnetic field (which is caused by electric currents flowing within the earth's liquid core) forces the atoms to line up in one direction.

Pierre Curie (husband of the famous chemist Marie Curie) discovered that there is a critical temperature (known as the "Curie temperature") beyond which the atoms of ferromagnets start to move around too much and lose their magnetism—this temperature alters for different metals. Iron (with a Curie temperature of 1,382 °F (750 °C)) forms a very strong magnet when heated to a glowing dull red. If the iron is then cooled very quickly it can be made into a permanent magnet. This explains why in the past, people found that an iron poker heated in a coal fire, became magnetic enough to pick up pieces of iron. Placing a ferromagnetic metal near to a strong magnet can also cause magnetism without the need for heat. This is how lightning magnetizes objects.

Large iron structures can become magnetic simply by being struck by lightning. When ships are made from iron they can become naturally magnetized in a storm.

During the Second World War, ships had to be demagnetized to prevent detection and targeting by bombs or mines. This was done by passing an enormous coil of wire around the ship and using electricity to make all the atoms point in different directions again.

A CAR USES ABOUT HALF ITS FUEL TO OVERCOME WIND RESISTANCE

Can you imagine a world without cars? Cars have become increasingly common on our roads over the last 100 years. But the rising cost of fuel means that car design has become more and more important. While older cars tend to be big and bulky, newer models have become sleek and streamlined. Car designers use their knowledge of physics to make vehicles that need less fuel to move longer distances.

THE SCIENCE OF...

A car traveling along a flat road needs to use fuel for energy, to overcome the force of friction so that it keeps moving. A car has two main sources of friction—the wheels, gears, and pistons moving in the engine, and the resistance of wind that moves over the surface of the car.

Car designers try to balance things out so that the car will lose about half its energy to each source when it is traveling at its "average speed." The gear box in a car keeps the engine speed roughly constant to reduce mechanical loss when the car speeds up. The wind resistance is quite small for a modern car traveling at average speed, but it increases rapidly at speeds of more than 50 mph (80 km/h). Making a car aerodynamic in shape reduces the amount of wind resistance—the designers of a Formula One racing car, which travels at up to 186 mph (300 km/h), work hard to reduce the wind resistance by giving the car a streamlined shape.

Brakes are also a major cause of energy loss when you are driving around town. Braking is a form of friction used to slow a car down and you have to use the car's engine to speed up again. Lots of stopping and starting requires more fuel or energy than a journey at a constant speed.

VOWZSAT!

DRIVING WITH THE CAR WINDOWS OPEN USES MORE FUEL THAN USING AIR CONDITIONING (WITH THE WINDOWS CLOSED). OPEN CAR WINDOWS CAUSE TURBULENCE WHEN MOVING AT SPEEDS OF MORE THAN 40 MPH (65KM/H)—AND EXTRA FUEL IS REQUIRED TO MAINTAIN SPEED.

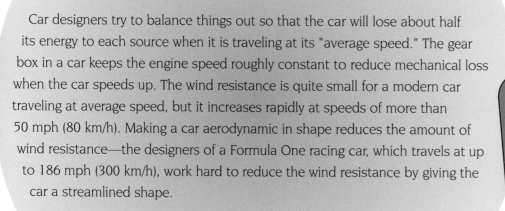

HOW DO WE KNOW?

Friction is produced whenever two materials move past each other. The moving parts of a modern engine have oil between them to prevent any rough surfaces rubbing together. Oil flows easily over the engine parts and absorbs less energy than a rough metal surface.

Car manufacturers use wind tunnels to simulate the conditions of air when a car is moving at different speeds. Air moving over a car flows easily but, if the air is forced to change direction very quickly, fast and slow moving air mix together. This produces "turbulence"—the main cause of wind resistance—and can affect fuel economy. Car manufacturers look at ways in which vehicle design can reduce wind resistance (or "drag").

Wind tunnels use a stream of air (injected with smoke to make it clearly visible) so that car designers can see where air flow causes resistance.

WHEN GLASS BREAKS, THE CRACKS MOVE AT 0.9 MILES (1.5 KM) PER SECOND

We've all broken something by mistake—and been shocked at the way in which a glass shatters or a dry twig suddenly "snaps." The way in which a material breaks is due to its structure. Materials like glass are brittle and they break very easily because they are unable to absorb the energy of a sudden force or impact.

THE SCIENCE OF...

The speed at which objects break varies for different types of materials. In a brittle material, like glass, cracks travel unhindered at around 4,920 feet per second (1,500 m/s)—a third of the speed of sound in that material. Brittle materials fracture because they are unable to absorb the energy that comes with impact—instead, all the energy is concentrated in one area and the cracks travel quickly. In contrast, flexible materials spread the force and energy of impact and small cracks don't spread. In a complicated material, like green wood, energy is absorbed in producing hundreds of new tiny cracks. That's why a green stick will splinter (left) as more and more cracks form.

Fibers like Kevlar, a strong substance used to make items such as bulletproof vests, are designed to absorb the energy of a high-speed bullet and tear like green wood. Modern plastics are often combined with fibers to stop cracks traveling right the way through the material. Boats, cars, and airplanes are all now made from a lightweight material called GRP (glass-reinforced plastic). Plastic is usually quite brittle but the addition of long, flexible fibers of glass makes it more flexible. Similarly, carbon fibers are added to steel in jet engine blades to make them less likely to break.

WOWZSAT!

DIAMONDS ARE CUT BY MAKING A CRACK BY SCRATCHING AND THEN OPENING THE CRACK WITH A KNIFE. THE SPEED OF SOUND IN DIAMONDS IS ABOUT 7.5 MILES PER SECOND (12 KM/S)—IT TAKES A MILLIONTH OF A SECOND FOR A CRACK TO SLICE THROUGH AN AVERAGE-SIZED DIAMOND!

How do we know?

High-speed photography has enabled us to follow the motion of cracks in different types of material. Photographs have shown that when a glass is broken, the stiffness of the glass concentrates all the force at the tip of the crack. Because the glass cannot absorb the energy elsewhere, the crack expands quickly and the glass fractures.

The speed of sound in glass is much higher than the speed of sound in air. Since the crack is traveling faster than the speed of sound in air, the breaking glass produces what is called a shockwave or sonic boom! The mini sonic boom is what we hear as the SNAP! or CRACK! of a breaking glass.

The old myth that an opera singer can break a glass with the sound of her voice is almost certainly true—but it's very difficult to actually achieve. Firstly, the glass in question needs to be made of crystal glass (glass that has had lead added to it). Crystal glass absorbs less vibrations than ordinary glass. If you gently tap a wineglass it produces a high-pitched tone. This is the "natural frequency" of the glass. If a singer uses her voice at the same frequency (or pitch), the vibrating air will start the glass vibrating too. And if the sound is of a sufficient volume the glass will try to vibrate farther and faster, and eventually the glass will shatter under the strain.

DIAMONDS ARE THE HARDEST OBJECTS IN THE WORLD

The word "diamond" comes from the Greek word "adamas," which means "invincible." The diamond is the hardest substance known to man. The chemical and physical properties of diamonds give this mineral a superior beauty and durability. Around 20 percent of the diamonds mined annually are highly sought after for the jewelry trade. The other 80 percent are used extensively in industry—to cut, grind, and to polish hard substances.

THE SCIENCE OF...

A diamond might get crushed if it were run over by a tank, but if it survived it would certainly remain unscratched! One of the most important properties of diamonds is that they are very hard. But hardness does not mean the same thing as "strength"—it all depends on whether we are squashing or stretching an object. Diamonds are very hard but they are not the strongest objects in the world —if you stretch a diamond it will snap like a piece of glass, just as an elastic band can be squashed without breaking, but will snap if you stretch it.

Diamonds are an unusual form of carbon that usually comes in the form of graphite —the material from which charcoal and pencil "leads" are made. If diamonds are the hardest objects in the world, how do you cut a diamond? A natural, or rough, diamond is first examined to decide where to cut it. It is then scratched by another diamond, and cracked by a steel knife, with a reinforced diamond cutting edge. In decorative jewelry, diamonds are cut a number of times and polished so that multiple reflective surfaces give the jewel its sparkle. Diamonds can also be manufactured synthetically from carbon —which is a cheaper alternative to extraction by mining. Synthetic diamonds are now used extensively in industry to produce long-lasting cutting tools such as saw blades and drills.

WOWZSAT!

DIAMONDS WERE DISCOVERED ABOUT 2,000 YEARS AGO IN INDIA BUT THE DIAMONDS THEMSELVES ARE MILLIONS OF YEARS OLD. SCIENTISTS BELIEVE THAT DIAMONDS ARE FORMED SOME 124 MILES (200 KM) BENEATH THE EARTH'S SURFACE.

STOP PRESS: In 1985, scientists discovered a third form of carbon that they called Fullerene. In 1997, it was discovered that by compressing Fullerene under intense pressure and at high temperatures, a new type of Fullerene, called "Ultrahard Fullerite," could be made. Recent experiments suggest that Ultrahard Fullerite can scratch diamond and so, perhaps, in the coming years diamond may no longer be classified as the hardest material in the world!

HOW DO WE KNOW?

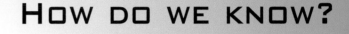

It is quite easy to tell if one material is harder than another—the hardest material is one that can't be scratched by any other. In 1822, Friedrich Mohs took ten materials and developed a scale of comparison. Mohs' "scale of hardness" is based on natural minerals (rocks that can be found in the ground):

10	Diamond	5	Apatite
9	Corundum	4	Fluorspar
8	Topaz	3	Calcite
7	Quartz	2	Gypsum
6	Feldspar	1	Talc

Today, we continue to use Mohs' scale of hardness to compare other everyday materials:

5.5	Glass
5.0	Steel
3.2	Copper
2.5 - 4.0	Pearls
2.2	Your fingernail

THE SCIENCE OF...

Most materials shrink when we cool them (see page 28). However, water behaves very differently between 32 °F and 39 °F (0-4° C). A water molecule (H_2O) is made from two hydrogen atoms bonded (or "stuck") to one oxygen atom, with the hydrogen atom of one molecule attracted to the oxygen atom of a neighboring molecule. In liquid water, the molecules slide past each other as the molecules join, break apart, and rejoin. When water cools, the molecules move more slowly and create more permanent attachments when they approach each other. The molecules in ice are held rigidly apart in a crystal structure and the water expands because there is more space between the molecules. When ice melts, the molecules move faster, break apart, and the water contracts as it "falls" into the gaps.

Ice has a lower density than water because water expands when it freezes. This is why icefloes and icebergs float on the surface of the sea.

ICE SKATERS SKATE ON WATER

A block of ice can be as rough as concrete, but an ice skater can travel for tens of feet with a single push. How can this be? The answer lies in how water behaves when we squeeze it. Unlike nearly every other common substance, water expands when it turns from a liquid into a solid. When the weight of an ice skater puts pressure onto an ice rink, the ice contracts and melts creating a slippery surface on which to glide.

HOW DO WE KNOW?

Simple experiments have helped to reveal the unusual properties of water. If you take a piece of ice that is just below its freezing point (32 °F / 0°C) and squeeze it, it melts! Similarly, when you stand on ice, the pressure of your body weight melts the surface and liquid flows out from beneath your feet. If the pressure is removed, refreezing occurs as the molecules rejoin.

When you put ice under pressure, the crystalline structure of the water is crushed, the joined molecules are broken apart, and the ice melts as the molecules start to move again. Ice skaters put a lot of pressure on an ice rink because their body weight is concentrated onto a pair of thin, smooth metal rails. Their weight causes a thin film of water to form on the ice, making it very slippery! Pressure effectively lowers the freezing point of ice—if you add a pressure 100 times that of normal atmospheric pressure, the freezing point of ice is lowered from 32 °F to 30 °F (0 °C to -1 °C).

The way in which pressure makes ice melt is also what enables you to make snowballs. Snowflakes are jagged and pointed, but when we take a handful of snow and squeeze it together the pressure causes the ice to melt. When we release the pressure the liquid freezes again, sticking the flakes together. If the snow is very cold (below about 5 °F, or -15 °C) it may not be possible to squeeze hard enough to make the ice melt. In this case when you let go of the snowball it simply falls apart again. That's why "wet" or warmer snow makes better snowballs!

How do we know?

Three temperature scales are in use today. The Fahrenheit (°F) scale is based on 32 °F for the freezing point of water and 212 °F for the boiling point of water. The Celsius/Centigrade (°C) scale is based on 0 °C for the freezing point of water and 100 °C for the boiling point of water. Today in science, we use the Kelvin (K) scale. This scale is the same as the Celsius scale except that its zero point is at -273 °C which we call "Absolute Zero."

Although it is impossible to reach Absolute Zero, scientists have conducted experiments that come very close. Methods include the use of magnets and evaporation techniques, and laser treatments. Cold atoms can be trapped by magnets and by removing any "hot" atoms that escape, scientists can cool an already cold substance even further. Scientists have discovered that atoms also slow down (and cool) when they are subjected to laser treatments. The lowest temperature ever produced is one thousandth of one millionth of a degree above Absolute Zero.

NOTHING CAN BE COLDER THAN -459 °F (-273 °C)

Most of us have an idea of the varying temperatures that occur in the world around us. A nice day is about 68 °F (20°C). Above 86 °F (30°C) it's very warm, and once above 98.6 °F (37°C) the air is hotter than our bodies and it's very difficult to stay cool. Below 32 °F (0°C) it's literally freezing cold. It may be difficult to imagine anything as cold as -459 °F (-273°C), but scientists now know that this is the coldest possible temperature!

THE SCIENCE OF...

Temperature is a measure of how much energy something has inside it. Heat, a form of energy, makes atoms move around and the faster they are moving, the farther they rebound when they bump into each other. If you cool a gas down, it shrinks in volume as the atoms and molecules of the gas move more slowly. Because this reduction in volume happens in a very predictable way scientists have been able to work out how cold a gas would have to be in order for the atoms to stop moving and the volume to be zero. This temperature (-459 °F / -273 °C) is the same for all gases. In reality, a gas will never reach this state, because as it cools it eventually changes from a gas to a liquid and shrinks more slowly. At -328 °F (-200 °C) the nitrogen and oxygen in the air around us become liquid, and by -364 °F (-220 °C) they become solid. By -436 °F (-260 °C) everything has become a solid except for the gas helium. It takes an astonishing -449 °F (-267 °C) to make helium into a liquid.

The coldest weather ever recorded on Earth was -128 °F (-89 °C), at Vostok, in Antarctica. This is extremely cold when you consider that the carbon dioxide that we breathe out freezes at -108 °F (-78 °C) to make "dry ice!" The chilly weather in Vostok is due to the exceptionally high speed of the Antarctic winds.

How do scientists cool something that is colder than the world around them? If you lick your finger and then blow on it, it gets colder even though your breath is as warm as your finger. This is because water molecules with the most energy evaporate, leaving behind water with less energy which is colder. Scientists use more sophisticated forms of this evaporation technique, using magnets to cool atoms to temperatures approaching Absolute Zero.

29

Glossary

Absolute Zero—The temperature at which substances possess no thermal energy (approximately -459 °F / -273 °C or 0 K).

Accelerate—To change speed or direction.

Aerodynamic—Designed to reduce wind resistance. Also known as "streamlined."

Atom—The smallest piece of a pure chemical element, e.g. hydrogen.

Brittle—Hard and easy to crack.

Crystal – The solid form of some substances in which atoms are regularly spaced.

Echo—A repeated sound formed when sound waves reflect off a flat surface.

Electricity—The movement of electrically charged particles.

Element—Substances that cannot be separated into simpler substances. Water is made from the elements hydrogen and oxygen.

Equator—An imaginary circle around the earth, halfway between the North and South Poles.

Evaporate—To change a liquid into a vapor by using heat or moving air.

Force—An effect that can change an object's speed, direction, or shape.

Freezing point—The temperature at which a liquid turns into a solid. The freezing point of a substance is also its melting point.

Friction—A force that slows down movement and produces heat, such as when two rough surfaces are rubbed together.

Gravity—The force that pulls all materials together across space.

Kilogram (kg)—The scientific unit of mass.

Magnetism—The property of some materials to attract or repel a piece of iron.

Mass—The amount of matter in an object.

Microscope—An instrument that uses magnifying lenses to make small objects appear larger.

Molecule—A particle made from two or more atoms of one or more elements.

Newton (N)—The scientific unit of force.

Optical illusion—Something that is visible but is not really as it seems.

Orbit—The path of an object as it travels around another object.

Prism—A triangular piece of glass used to bend rays of light and to split white light into different colors.

Reflection—When a beam of light is bounced off a surface, e.g. the reflection of light in a mirror.

Turbulence—The disturbance in a fluid or gas, usually caused by a solid body passing through it.

Vacuum—An empty space that doesn't contain any matter, air, or gas.

Weight—The force with which something is attracted to the earth. Weight is measured in newtons but we usually convert this to pounds or kilograms.

Biography

Henry Cavendish (1731-1810) A British physicist who worked out the value of the gravitational constant ("G").

Anders Celsius (1701-1744) A Swedish physicist who devised the Celsius temperature scale.

Pierre Curie (1859-1906) A French physicist and chemist whose work included studies on the properties of magnetism.

Daniel Gabriel Fahrenheit (1686-1736) A German physicist who invented the Fahrenheit temperature scale.

Galilei Galileo (1564-1642) An Italian scientist whose contributions to physics and astronomy included the study of motion.

Friedrich Mohs (1773-1839) A German mineralogist who devised the Mohs' scale for comparing the hardness of different substances.

Sir Isaac Newton (1642-1727) A British physicist who proposed three laws of forces and motion and a universal law of gravity for objects [Force of gravity = G x (Mass1/distance) x (Mass2/distance)].

William Thompson (Lord Kelvin) (1824-1907) A Scottish physicist who proposed a temperature scale, equivalent to the Celsius scale, but starting from Absolute Zero (now called the Kelvin scale).

Johannes Diderik van der Waals (1837-1923) A Dutch physicist who calculated the size of atoms by studying the way that gases behave when they are heated and compressed.

KEY DATES

1624—Galilei Galileo puts forward his theory of the ocean's tides.

1672—Isaac Newton publishes his studies on the spectrum of light.

1687—Isaac Newton publishes his laws of motion.

1709—Daniel Fahrenheit invents the alcohol thermometer.

1743—Anders Celsius establishes the Celsius temperature scale.

1798—Henry Cavendish measures the gravitational constant.

1848—William Thompson devises the Kelvin temperature scale.

1895—Pierre Curie discovers the temperature at which ferromagnets lose their magnetic properties.

Index

Photocredits:
Abbreviations: l-left, r-right, b-bottom, t-top, c-center, m-middle. Front cover l, back cover r, 12tr, 18-19, 31mr – Corbis. 4br, 8mr – Charles M. Duke Jr./NASA. 24mr – Corel. 5tr, 24-25 – Lance Cpl. Samuel Bard Valliere/USMC. 5mrt, 14-15 – Iconotec. 5mrb, 6br, 18bm, 20mr, 22ml, 26t – Photodisc. 5br, 8-9, 18b, 26bl, 28-29, 30br – Digital Stock. 9bl – Flick Smith. 9ml, 29br – PBD. 9br – Dr James P. McVey/NOAA Sea Grant Program. 12l – Brand X Pictures. 17bl – Roger Vlitos. 21 – National Research Council, Canada. 22-23 – with thanks to Pilkington Building Products-UK.